SADIE

GOES TO CAMP

WRITTEN BY
LINDA ZIMMERMAN

ILLUSTRATED BY
NEIL McMILLIN

To Sadie, you are my inspiration, and will always have a special place in my heart.

To the many individuals who are dedicated to helping rescues and shelters provide compassionate care to pets waiting for their forever homes.

"I am packed and ready to go," says Annie.

"Are you packed Sadie?" asks Mom.

"Almost," I answer.

Annie yells, "Sadie! You can't take all that stuff. And you can't take Gracie!"

"It is only a few things." I reply. "Just what I need for the week."

Annie rolls her eyes and says, "You only need a toothbrush, sunglasses, and a doggie towel. You need to repack!"

Annie and I are finally on our way to CAMP BARK-A-LOT. I will miss Mom, Dad, and Gracie, but I can't wait to meet new friends and go swimming and hiking. Oh, and roasting hot dogs over a campfire. Yum! Yum!

Since this is my first year at camp in wheels, Justin, the camp director, thinks I could use a buddy. He introduces me to Juliana. She is sweet and smells like marshmallows.

**On our first day, we take a short hike in the morning.
I love walking in the woods in my wheels.**

In the afternoon, we take a swim in the lake. But the water is so C O L D! Brr!

"I think I see a polar bear!" Annie says as she dog-paddles.

My teeth are chattering. "I'm shivering so much I think I see tw-tw-two!"

Our second day, we have arts and crafts. I am so artistic! But I ate my macaroni necklace. I couldn't help myself. It was tasty!

That night we roast hot dogs and marshmallows.

Oh my, I ate too many marshmallows!

The next morning at breakfast, I am called to Justin's office. Annie looks at me with disapproving eyes. "I *told* you not to eat that macaroni necklace!" she says.

"I guess I am in trouble," I say in a low voice.

"No, Sadie, you aren't the first camper to eat your art project." Justin says. "Did you know that each summer, a few dogs from the local rescue attend our camp?"

"I did not know," I say. "That is really awesome!"

"Yes, but one of the dogs, Patch, is a five-year-old pit bull, and he is having a difficult time adjusting to camp." Justin says. "Would you talk to Patch and try to help him?"

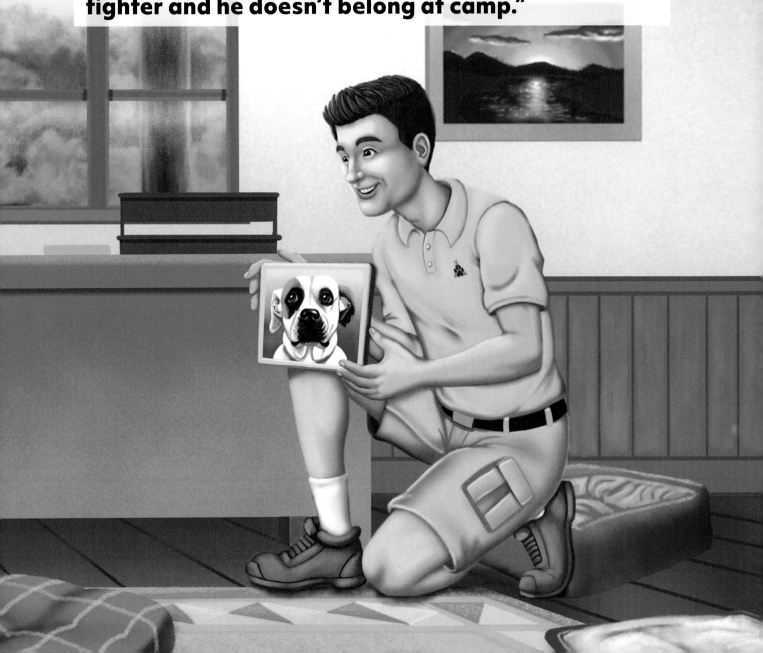

"Yes, yes. I would love to meet Patch," I reply.

"Patch has a damaged ear," Justin adds, "and he is afraid that will make the other dogs think he is a fighter and he doesn't belong at camp."

I find Patch in his cabin, staring out the window. He looks sad. "Hi!" I say. "I am Sadie, and I am so happy to meet you. Can you come out and play?"

"Hello, I am Patch," he replies. "I don't think the other campers want me to play. They think because I have a funny ear, I like to fight."

"Patch, there are campers who will love you if you let them." I say. "Don't worry about your ear. I have wheels because my legs are weak, and everyone accepts me just as I am."

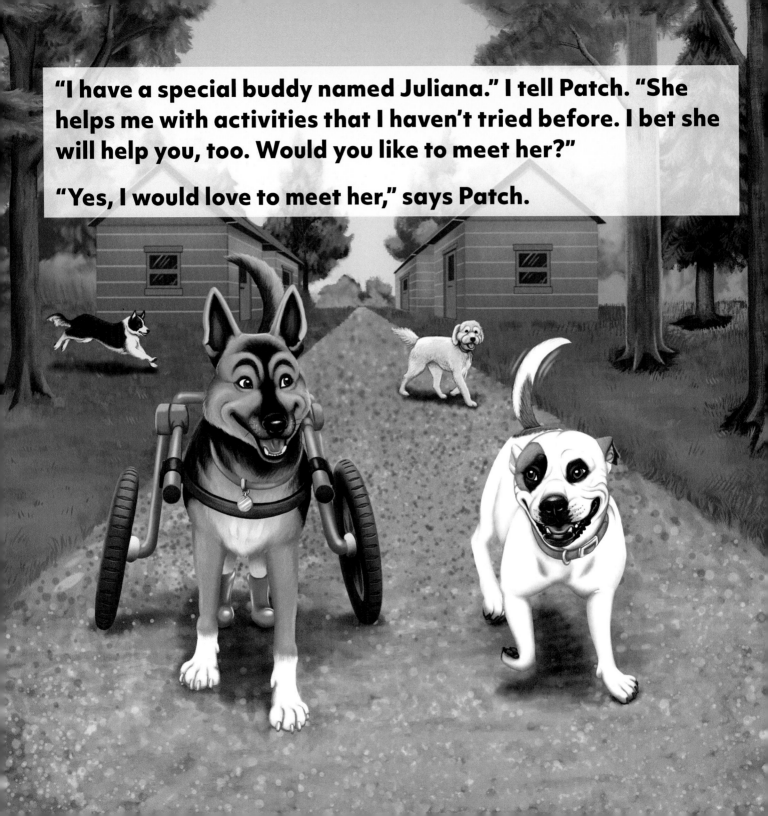

"I have a special buddy named Juliana." I tell Patch. "She helps me with activities that I haven't tried before. I bet she will help you, too. Would you like to meet her?"

"Yes, I would love to meet her," says Patch.

"Hi, Patch!" Juliana says. "May I be your buddy?"

" I would like to be your buddy," Patch says shyly, "but I am a rescue dog with no family so I'm not sure how."

Juliana smiles. "I'll show you! I bet you'll be a great buddy and you will be adopted someday. Now, let's go and play."

At bedtime, I say a special prayer that Patch will have lots of fun at camp and that someday, he will meet his forever family.

Today, I got a postcard from Gracie. She says she misses me. I miss her, too!

Patch is having so much fun playing, boating, and fishing.

I was right; the campers all love Patch once they get to know him.

In arts and crafts class, Patch makes a beautiful macaroni necklace, and he does not eat it.

What a great week! The last night of camp, we eat ice cream sundaes with lots of chocolate syrup, whipped cream, and cherries. DELICIOUS!

It is time to go home. I will be happy to see my mom, dad, and Gracie, but I am sad to say good-bye to all my new friends, especially Juliana and Patch.

I tell Patch, that I will see him at camp next summer, but he says it will be another rescue dog's turn to come to camp. I tell him I will miss him, and I will visit him at the rescue.

I am sad watching Patch get ready to board the rescue bus and say good-bye to Juliana. But then something wonderful happens.

Juliana gives Patch a big hug, but it's not a good-bye hug. She tells him her parents say she can adopt him. Now he will have a forever family!

"What an awesome end to a wonderful week!" I say as Annie and I board the camp bus for home. "Like I told Patch, good people don't judge dogs by their looks or breed – or by their wheels!"

CAMP BARK-A-LOT

MY WHEELS OF WISDOM

Do not judge others by the way they look.

Remember, playing outdoors is great exercise and fun.

Open your heart to shelter and rescue pets.

NEVER, EVER, eat your macaroni necklace!

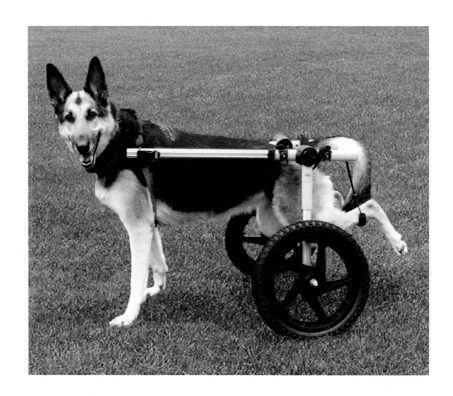

Meet Sadie, the inspiration for the *Sadie* book series. A friendly, and playful German Shepherd whose life changed suddenly when at the age of 8, she was diagnosed with Degenerative Myelopathy (DM). DM is a progressive disease that affects the spinal cord resulting in paralysis of the hind legs. There is no cure or proven treatment that can stop the progression of DM.

As Sadie's legs became weaker, she received a set of wheels. With her new wheels she was back playing, running and enjoying her daily walks. It was amazing the number of children and adults who wanted to know more about this dog in wheels. It was on these walks that the author realized that Sadie had a story to share.